Robb
Al

ORCA BOOK PUBLISHERS

National Library of Canada Cataloguing in Publication Data
Sander, Heather, 1947-

Robbie Packford--alien monster / Heather Sander.

ISBN 1-55143-259-5

I. Title.

PS8587.A327R62 2003   jC813'.6   C2003-910881-3

PZ7.S1975Ro 2003

Library of Congress Catalog Card Number: 2003107508

Summary: Fantasy/science fiction. Robbie Packford was an ordinary
grade six boy, but now he is an alien monster, soon to be transported to
Kerbosky, where only he can save an enslaved planet.

Teachers' guide available at www.orcabook.com

Orca Book Publishers gratefully acknowledges the support of its
publishing programs provided by the following agencies: the
Department of Canadian Heritage, the Canada Council for the Arts,
and the British Columbia Arts Council.

Cover design by Christine Toller
Cover & interior illustrations by Cindy Revell
Printed and bound in Canada

IN CANADA	IN THE UNITED STATES
Orca Book Publishers	Orca Book Publishers
1030 North Park Street	PO Box 468
Victoria, BC Canada	Custer, WA USA
V8T 1C6	98240-0468

05 04 03 • 5 4 3 2 1

To Brandon and Chase,
dear grandchildren and our future.

Chapter One

I was still human, but barely.

I glanced down at my fingers. They had curved into claws, sharp claws, the kind that could rend and tear.

I tapped a claw against my teeth. Wow! Fangs, sharp as rapiers. Nibbling was out. Tearing and slashing were in.

Come to think of it, I was starting to feel hungry. I propelled my body across the kitchen, my armored tail flicking in anticipation. My claws grasped the fridge handle. At least they still worked like hands, well, sort of. Greedily, my eyes feasted on the contents of the fridge. Ugh and yuck to the tofu Mom had bought for Aunt Rose. Forget the carrots. Forget the chips and dip.

Ahhh! My eyes lighted upon it. Saliva dribbled from the corners of my mouth. My claws grasped. My teeth tore. Now this was real food. A glorious burp rumbled up from my stomach. Then I thought to myself in horror: You've just eaten the family roast — raw!

This was becoming a nightmare. I was transforming into some horrible creature with fangs and claws and a tail, a creature who had devoured the family roast and was thinking about how his little sister might taste for dessert.

"Help," I said, but all that came out was a growl. Now I was really scared. The human part of me was shrinking smaller and smaller. My own voice inside my hideous body was like a whisper, then an echo.

Hold on to who you are; hold on, I told myself desperately. More thoughts of raw oozing meat engulfed my mind. This wasn't me. This couldn't be me. Maybe if I breathed very slowly the nightmare would go away. Maybe if I reviewed how this thing had happened — there had to be a solution.

I'm not a horror movie that leaped off the screen into real life. I'm me, Robbie Packford, the kid with glasses from down the street, my nose always in a book, useless at baseball. But just ask me the stats of the National Hockey League and I can reel them off. I'm not interested in weird, meat-eating monsters. I missed the dinosaur fascination stage. I like learning about spaceflight, early humans and the law of probability. But this time that very law had done me in.

A flood of memories swept through my brain, temporarily pushing aside the need for raw meat. I must have been crazy. Maybe I still was crazy. I clacked my claws together where I used to have fingers. Still there, sharp as ever.

It all started so simply with this new kid in my class. Who would have thought that some new kid at school who said he was really an alien could have been telling the truth? What are the odds of that, one in ten gazillion? I'd call that the law of extreme improbability. When he, Jamie the alien (but, of course, I didn't know that then), gave me the formula to drink, I just laughed.

I bashed my claws to my scaly forehead. It was getting harder to think. Reptilian thoughts invaded my brain, images of raw meat and dank caves. I thought about sharpening my claws on the furniture, nibbling on family members.

Think, I growled deep within myself, think human.

When Jamie came to our class, I thought it might be cool to be his friend. Well, not actually cool, more like an insurance policy against teasing. Sometimes it pays to have a friend who's a bigger weirdo than you are. I know that sounds really self-serving, but us geeks get desperate sometimes. Being advanced in math usually isn't the best basis for friendship.

Anyhow, Jamie kept saying that he was this alien who had escaped from some war on a faraway planet. Yeah, right. And how *they* might be coming to get him. He didn't exactly say who. All he had was this formula that would make him invincible. It wasn't finished when he escaped, but he thought a few Earth ingredients could be substituted.

That's how we ended up in the basement with a bunch of stuff from Mom's kitchen — baking powder, food coloring. It was a fun kind of fantasy. Who wouldn't like to be invincible?

Jamie told me to try it first. I laughed, but he was pretty convincing in his geek-like way, charming actually. So what the heck, I tried it.

At first I didn't feel any different, just a little hungry. Then Jamie's eyes began to bug out. I thought he was putting me on. I was going to say, "Stop it, Jamie, now you're scaring me," when my skin began to feel tight all over and these scaly things began to pop out all over my body. Then the claws began and the fangs.

Jamie was saying something like, "No, no, it's all wrong," and I was thinking about screaming or fainting, I didn't know which, when there was this beam of light. Sparkling blue. It cooled the basement and made Jamie's face look sick. The light encircled Jamie. His mouth moved, but no sounds came out. He kept pointing up. I stepped towards him and *poof*, with a gush of wind someone turned the blue light off. The problem was, when the blue blinked out it took Jamie with it.

The rest was the nightmare that wouldn't stop, where I got to the kitchen and ate the meat and started to think how my little sister might taste. I would have pinched myself to see if I was dreaming if I could have, but claws aren't good at that. I slouched my way through the kitchen and looked out the window. Mary, my sister, was still out there skipping with her bratty friends. She turned towards the window. I ducked. I couldn't let her see me like this. Who knew when the desire to eat her would overcome me? Was I still her big brother or was I just this awful monster?

I lumbered up the stairs to check myself out in the hall mirror. The sight that greeted me would have made me faint in terror if I were still a boy. The thing that looked back at me from the mirror was approximately the same size as the late Robbie Packford. But that was all. Any remaining similarity to any human living or dead would have been purely accidental. I had a snout and fangs. I was green-brown and blotched with scales everywhere. I had evil little red eyes that stared at me from under bony brows, and a tail that could smash the TV into smithereens with one sweep. I probably even had bad breath. The only good thing was that the new me

still walked upright and had claws that could grasp things.

I collapsed in a heap before the mirror. How could I get back to being Robbie Packford? I'd do anything to be my nerdie self, glasses perched on the end of my nose, reading a book and not hearing when Mom called me for supper. I groaned a monster groan and wondered if monsters could cry. I even tried to make tears come out of my deep-set evil red eyes.

I have to find Jamie, I thought. He did this. There must be a way to get back to being human. Recklessly, I searched the basement. All that was left of the formula was a broken glass and no trace of Jamie. He had disappeared, leaving me to live out the rest of my days as a miserable monster. Just as I was feeling really sorry for myself, I heard a noise in the driveway. Oh, no. Mom was home. I had to get out of here. I dived for the back door, wondering if monsters gobbled their own parents for supper.

Chapter Two

Again the monster was hungry. It slunk through the alleyways, avoiding the bright lights. It lifted its green snout to smell the air. Its armored tail thrashed in the darkness. Need to eat, thought the monster. In the far recesses of its brain was a memory. No, even less than that, a thought like a puff of smoke, disappearing. It had not always been as it was now. Somewhere there was another life, another thought pattern. The monster shook its head and the niggling thought evaporated, to be replaced by the gnawing desire to feed. There was a rule in the monster's brain. It could not understand the words of the rule or where it had come from. The rule said, Do not eat living things. Do not eat people, dogs or cats. But why not? Where had the rule come from?

People looked and smelled juicy enough, tender and good.

Eat, need to eat, repeated the monster's brain. The monster slouched down the dim alley, its keen sense of smell guiding it to the garbage cans behind the dark houses. Strong claws ripped off the lids and flung them with a clang to the road. Into the can went the snout, fangs opening, searching through the debris for the remnants of meat. When it lifted its bony head, green saliva dribbled from its fangs and its beady red eyes glinted in the light of the crescent moon. Even after the entire block of garbage bins had been ravaged and lay scattered, a storm of dented cans and littered wrappers, the monster knew it needed more. The food in these unguarded bins was not enough to keep the monster strong. Fresh meat, fresh kill. Only that would satisfy.

The monster raised its head. Appealing odors greeted its flared nostrils, the overpowering scent of food. Abruptly it turned, poised against danger. Then a noise. "Robbie," called a voice, but to the monster it was only a grunt. But strange. That noise, the sound of it seemed familiar as if the monster should recognize it. Slowly the monster turned its head. Saliva dripped from its jaws.

The sound came again, the one the monster should know. But now its need for food was overpowering. Beside the garbage cans stood two figures, one about the same size as the monster, but slight, and the other one a little bigger. That one looked bony and old. The monster rejected it in favor of the smaller one. Juicy meat, fresh kill, thought the monster, advancing towards the still figure.

Now the figure cried out to him. "Robbie Packford, don't you recognize me? It's me, Jamie, Jamie — your friend from school. Don't you remember the formula?"

The figure stepped back one step, shaking. The monster heard the noises from the figure's mouth, but they made no sense. Only the monster's overwhelming need for food mattered. The giant jaws opened, revealing a line of gleaming fangs. The figure screamed and fell backwards.

Suddenly the monster glimpsed a movement from the side. "Here, catch," cried the second figure, the scrawny, bony one that would probably taste tough. Instinctively the monster snapped its jaws shut on the thrown object. Something soft and gooey hit the back of its tongue. The monster gave a slurp and a burp and paused.

Not enough food, thought the monster. Before him the fresh meat shook, waiting for the jaws to close.

"Robbie, Robbie, don't you know me? Stop!" cried the voice.

Abruptly, the monster stopped, just as its powerful jaws readied themselves to slam shut like a steel trap. The cries from the figure had begun to make sense.

"Jamie," growled the monster. "It's you."

"Thank the stars," shouted the older figure. "I thought we were goners. I wasn't certain the new formula would work until this instant. At least we're not dinner."

Dinner, thought the monster, who suddenly remembered that its name was actually Robbie Packford and that up until now he had been a pretty ordinary kid in the sixth grade. With a wave of dizziness it all came back. I was Robbie again and I could think for myself.

Jamie was the new boy at our school who had said he was an alien and had given me the formula, the formula that had turned me into . . . *the monster inhabiting my body who had been about to eat my new friend for dinner*! That was not what Mrs. Cardwell had in mind when she gave the class talks about welcoming new kids to the class. Showing them where the gym and computer room were was one thing, but munching and crunching them with your terrible fangs was another.

I shuddered. "I'm sorry. I don't know what came over me."

"Perfectly understandable under the circumstances," replied the second figure. I stared at him. He was awfully short for a grown-up and had curly white hair sprouting all over the top of his head. At the end of his very long nose wiggled a pair of pince-nez. He had a white coat on, the kind that scientists wear. In fact, with his unruly white hair and glinting eyes he did look a bit like a mad scientist.

"Who are you?" I growled.

"Allow me to introduce myself," declared

the old man, revealing gleaming white teeth that matched his hair. "I am Dr. Freedelhum, a friend of Jamie, and from the same planet as well." He smiled again, bowing with a flourish.

"I take it you are not talking about the planet Earth," I snarled dryly.

"My goodness, no," returned Dr. Freedelhum. "We are visiting from the planet Kerbosky."

Wow, I thought, and people used to want to go to Mexico or Australia for vacations. Maybe visiting Earth was the new intergalactic rage. A good deal, off the beaten track, at the edge of an arm of the Milky Way. Why not?

But instead of saying all this, what I actually said was, "You have to turn me back into a boy. You don't know how close you came to being devoured."

Dr. Freedelhum bowed again. "There is a tiny problem with that, but one that we will have quickly ironed out. Not to worry."

It was okay for Dr. Freedelhum to say that. He hadn't just ransacked twenty garbage cans eating who knows what disgusting garbage. And he hadn't just about devoured two people (change that to aliens) for dinner. I could not believe this. Here I was in the middle of the night with the body of a monster, lashing my scaly armored tail, talking to two aliens. I wished I could wake up from this nightmare and find myself safe in my room with the comforting blinking light from the computer.

"What's the catch?" I asked suspiciously. "Monsters are okay, but only in movies."

"Well, you see, my young friend," said the doctor, "with the Earth ingredients he used, Jamie accidentally changed the nature of the formula very slightly. Plus, using it on humans, whose internal physiology is slightly different from our own . . . Well, I'm certain you understand."

"All I understand," I growled, "is that I hate being a monster and who knows when I might decide to eat you."

Dr. Freedelhum snapped open his briefcase and produced another gooey blob like the one he had thrown to the monster. "As long as we have a supply of this, your human personality will not be totally submerged."

"I don't want my human personality

unsubmerged," I wailed. "I want me back."

Dr. Freedelhum snapped the briefcase shut. "Are all humans this impatient?" he asked Jamie.

Jamie shrugged. "Dunno," he said. "I wasn't here long enough. All that happened to me was that three people tripped me on the playground and the girls called me a nerd."

Some help you are, I thought. "Why did you tell me to drink that stupid formula?"

"I'm sorry, Robbie. I really am. I thought it would work. I was sure, well, practically sure, but I guess I goofed up big time."

I was about to reply when Dr. Freedelhum held up his hand. "No time now for small talk," he said. "You boys can chat later. We have to go."

"Go?" I croaked. "Go where?"

"To our spaceship, of course," replied Dr. Freedelhum. "I'll just adjust the molecular teleporter for a human — er — I mean monster, and we'll be off."

"Wait!" I yelled. "I don't want to go in any spaceship. My socials report is due on Friday. I've already missed my swimming lesson and . . ."

Dr. Freedelhum smiled his irritating smile and shrugged. "Well it's either come with us or stay a monster forever."

I gulped. It wasn't much of a choice. As the blue light enveloped us and I felt my molecules begin to shimmer and waver, I whispered sadly into the black night, "Good-bye, Earth."

Chapter Three

"Very interesting," murmured Dr. Freedelhum, bringing up more information on the computer screen. "In fact, fascinating. Jamie, my boy, this might well be a scientific coup. And Robbie —" The doctor pointed to a glob of the brown goo beside the computer desk. "It's time for your portion of Glicko Goo. Twice a day should be sufficient."

My fangs closed on the goo, which hit the back of my throat like fizzy pop. "What if we run out?" I gagged.

"Not to worry," said Dr. Freedelhum. "We can always whip some up in the automatic molecular food processor. Just feed the instructions into the computer and, presto, there you have it."

"Yeah, Robbie," interrupted Jamie. "We can make anything we want to eat. Now that you've got your personality back, you might prefer normal human food."

"As opposed to raw meat?" I shuddered.

Jamie grinned. "Why don't you order some up now. Look, I've programmed in all the fast-food restaurants in the world. There are ninety-seven different pizza chains alone, and one thousand and seventeen hamburger joints."

Dr. Freedelhum patted Jamie on the head. "He's our boy genius," he admitted, "a computer whiz, but while you are deciding on the menu, let me show you something. Come closer."

Dr. Freedelhum scrolled up the computer by pointing his finger at the screen. I stared. Beside the print in some weird language that didn't look like anything I'd ever seen before was a picture, a picture of me. Oh, I don't mean a picture of Robbie Packford like the ones they take on photo days that you send copies of to your grandparents for Christmas; no, I mean ME, the now me, the monster me. I gasped.

"Amazing," commented Dr. Freedelhum, squinting through his pince-nez at the squiggly writing on the screen. "It seems your famous formula, Jamie, has turned our friend into a mythical creature from dim eons past. In fact, scientists never even believed that it existed."

Until now, I thought.

"Until now," repeated Dr. Freedelhum, as if reading my mind. "And it seems this mythical creature had some very unusual powers. But order up your supper, boys, while I finish this paragraph. Jamie, would you mind ordering me one of those Earth cappuccinos and the round flat thing with cheese and tomato sauce on it — what was it called?"

"Pizza," returned Jamie.

"Yes," said Dr. Freedelhum, "make mine with everything."

"Pizza sounds good," I grunted, beginning to salivate through my fangs. "Pizza for me, too, but hold the olives and the onions. I hate them both."

"Coming right up," answered Jamie, pressing some buttons on the molecular food-processing computer. Suddenly a lovely pizza smell wafted out of the machine and a little door slid open, revealing three pizzas looking hot from the oven.

"How 'bout a shake with that?" asked Jamie.

"Make mine chocolate," I said, glad that I could eat human food again. All that horrible garbage I had devoured out of garbage cans — I was sure I'd have nightmares about it.

Jamie set the pizza before me and I began to wonder how monsters ate their food in polite company without tearing or rending. My claws were even stronger than I had imagined. The first piece of pizza was punctured by claw indentations. The second ripped to shreds before it could reach my salivating mouth. It landed with a plop on the shining white floor of the spacecraft.

Jamie grinned at me and held out another piece. "Slow and easy?" he asked. I nodded my monster head, spraying the computer console with a few droplets of monster drool. I concentrated on the pizza slice in Jamie's outstretched hand. Getting food into my mouth hadn't been a problem since I learned to use a spoon as a baby. Gingerly I put out my claws and clacked them together experimentally.

"You don't want to crush or tear," Jamie reminded me. "Think grasp lightly."

"Just lay it in my hand," I ordered. "I don't want to lop off bits of your fingers by mistake." Jamie laid the pizza slice in my open claws. I stared at it, slurping excess drool from my scaly chin with my tongue. I raised my hand — er — claw towards my mouth. I could easily eat my own claws when I bit the pizza. Not good. How did carnivorous dinosaurs do it? Gouts of saliva lolled off my jumbo purple tongue and onto the floor. Then, all on its own, my tongue snaked out of my mouth and knotted itself around the pizza slice. In one second the warm gooey cheese crust, tomato paste and toppings were sliding down my throat.

"Great!" Jamie said. "It will just take practice. Claws take some getting used to."

I don't want to get used to claws, I told myself. But if the only eating I was going to do was with claws and fangs, I had better get down to it. I skewered the next pizza piece with my claw and tried to nibble around the edges. Surprisingly, practice was helping and I managed the pizza with just a few reminders to myself to take small bites. After a while I even figured out how to drink the milkshake through the straw, although at first I kept getting my fangs and my tongue in the way. The last thing I wanted to do was bite my tongue by accident. I slurped the last of the pizza cheese off my claws. A long burp rumbled from my monster tummy, making the computer images waver. Jamie frowned and held his nose.

I was getting pretty good at the monster eating part! Computer pizza tasted just like Earth pizza. If I tried out a different fast food every day . . . Wait! That would take years. I was starting to think like I was going to be in this spaceship with Jamie and Dr. Freedelhum for a long time. Come to think of it, they hadn't said a word about getting me back to being human again.

"Earth food isn't half bad," said Dr. Freedelhum. "I think I'll try a latte next."

"Right," agreed Jamie. "Robbie, you should try the food from some of the other planets. Gross!"

"Can't be worse than garbage can remains," I grunted, dropping the milkshake cup on the floor beside the spattered remains of the pizza I'd just eaten. Monster eating was lesson number one. Eating without making your surroundings into a gooey, saliva-glutted mess would be number two. I burped again. Lesson number two could wait for another day. Jamie swept the remains into the molecular transformer.

"It works like magic," he said. "The molecules are transformed into other structures. Not an atom is ever wasted."

Cool, I thought, remembering how many times Dad had to remind me to take out the garbage or the recycling. A doubt niggled up against my monster brain. "How come you know so much about Earth food?" I asked suspiciously.

Dr. Freedelhum polished his already gleaming pince-nez on the sleeve of his immaculate lab coat. "Research," he answered.

"Research?" I echoed.

Jamie nodded. "Dr. Freedelhum's lifework is the researching of food on alien planets."

I nodded dumbly, shaking my scales as if this made sense. It didn't. "We were researching the planets in this sector for the next project when —" Jamie stopped, glancing at Dr. Freedelhum.

Even a monster could tell when he wasn't getting the whole story.

"Yes, yes," interrupted Dr. Freedelhum, "the Milky Way, a fascinating galaxy, so many worlds to explore, so many new recipes to discover." Dr. Freedelhum licked his thin lips with his pink tongue. His tongue was long and pointed as if it belonged to a lizard. "Don't you like the lab coat?" he demanded. "And my pince-nez?"

"Huh?" I asked.

"Earth fashions," added Jamie. It was then that I learned that even alien research had its flaws.

Dr. Freedelhum fiddled with the computer. Then he gestured towards me. He looked very excited. The pince-nez wavered up and down on his long nose. "Read this," he ordered.

I stared at the squiggles and at the picture of the new me — fangs, claws and even saliva. Very realistic.

"I'm sorry, I forgot," he said. "You'll need this." He handed me what looked like a tiny gold earring, the kind that they first put in when you get your ears pierced, a sleeper. "Just put it in your ear," he ordered. Then Dr. Freedelhum stared at me. "Say, where exactly are your ears?" he said.

I felt the sides of my head. Obviously I had ears. I could hear perfectly well. If anything, I could hear better than before. Where were they? Monster anatomy was a little different from human anatomy.

"Probably anywhere will do. Just stick it up against your skin — er — scales. Universal translators work with all known species. Some of them don't have external ears either. You'll be able to understand all the alien languages in our computer bank and read them, too."

"It's a computer chip," Jamie added, casting the remains of his dinner into the molecular transformer.

Doubtfully, I pushed the earring up against a brown scale where an ear should have been. I didn't feel anything, but somehow it attached. Jamie held up a mirror. I could see it, the glint of the tiny earring against the green and brown of my scales. A monster fashion statement! I turned to the computer screen. The squiggles had turned themselves into words.

"'Campythronagithicus Fabutali,'" I read aloud, "'a mythological creature of the planet

Kerbosky, known for its amazing and unusual powers and the nasty habit of devouring others.' Wow," I exclaimed. "It IS lucky I didn't eat you both. What does it say about unusual powers?"

Dr. Freedelhum scrolled up the printing. "'Many powers have been attributed to the beast,'" he read, "'including seeing through solid, objects, flight and the ability to disappear.'"

"Try it out," shouted Jamie. "Let's see you disappear. Just concentrate."

I concentrated. I squeezed my beady red eyes shut. I held my monster breath and thrashed my tail until I thought my eyes would pop out. Nothing happened. Dr. Freedelhum and Jamie looked disappointed.

"Well, you are a mythical creature and I imagine the tales about you must be exaggerated," murmured Dr. Freedelhum disapprovingly.

I frowned.

"But you are very powerful," Jamie said, giving my scales a pat. "We'll call you Campy for short," he added.

"But only until you find a way to get

me back to being a boy," I insisted. "How long will that take, anyway?"

"If we could figure out the exact molecular components in the Earth products Jamie added to the formula, it would be simple to program it into the molecular processor and, presto, reverse the formula. It would take a bit of experimentation and time, but —"

"But," interrupted Jamie, "we have a bigger problem to deal with right now."

"You mean bigger than getting me back to being Robbie Packford before I flunk out of grade six?" I asked.

"Yep," said Dr. Freedelhum, nodding his head so violently that the white kinky curls shook all over. "And we can't solve it without your help."

"Exactly what is it you need me to do?" I asked, with a sinking feeling right down to the pit of my monster stomach.

Chapter Four

You know how it is. You're having one of those really bad days when you think not one more thing can go wrong. And then — you know what happens next. I couldn't believe what Jamie and Dr. Freedelhum were telling me. But here I was, standing in the control room of an alien spaceship. I was a monster with no chance of returning to Earth unless I helped them out. My beady red eyes roved the control room, watching the blinking lights.

"All we have to do is change the master instructions in the Nerve Center," Jamie said.

He was making our task sound simple, but it was probably going to be a nightmare.

"We could sneak you in, give you the code and, presto!" said Dr. Freedelhum. How

I was beginning to hate that word.

"If you could practice the invisibility part, that would help a lot, too," suggested Jamie.

My monster brain was reeling. It had been bad enough keeping track of things on Earth: socials reports, who to stay away from on the playground, that sort of thing. But all the stuff about wars and robots — it was too much for one monster brain to comprehend, even if that brain did have special powers (supposedly).

"It's simple," Jamie said. "All we have to do is change the Master Ordinance back to what it was in the Nerve Center."

"What's the Master Ordinance?" I said, more confused than ever.

"It's the basic rule for the robots who serve the people of Kerbosky," said Dr. Freedelhum, pushing buttons on the computer to change our orbit slightly. He had put us in an orbit around Earth's moon while they explained the problem to me. We were passing over it now. I could see the giant craters below us through the window dome. This was a lot better than our class field trip to the observatory!

"The Master Ordinance," said Jamie, "is

BE NICE; that's how robots are always supposed to act."

"Be nice!" I said. "That sounds like Mrs. Cardwell, my teacher, 'Why can't you just be nice to each other?'"

Dr. Freedelhum interrupted. "The problem is, the Master Ordinance has been changed. And now the robots are taking control."

"You mean they are trying to control your planet?"

"Not exactly," Dr. Freedelhum said with a frown. "They have already enslaved our planet. Now they want to control the universe."

"B . . . but," I stammered, lashing my tail in consternation.

"In fact," continued Dr. Freedelhum, "we are the only free people left from our planet, Jamie and me. Luckily, we were in the midst of the Milky Way Exotic Food Research Project when we received the last transmission from the citizens of our home planet before they were overpowered by the robots. We thought we'd come to a little-known, out-of-the-way part of the galaxy to make a plan to stop the robots. And since we were already researching the region around your solar system . . ."

"You mean there's just the three of us?" I was dumbfounded. "How many robots would you say we were up against?"

"Maybe around four billion," Dr. Freedelhum said, "but that's not really the point."

"It's not the point that two kids and a scientist, I mean one kid, one monster without unusual powers and a scientist, are up against billions of robots who don't want to be nice anymore?"

Dr. Freedelhum patted my armored head. "Well, Campy," he said, "it's like this. Issuing new instructions to the Nerve Center would change all those robots back just the way they used to be, friendly and helpful."

"What are they like now?"

"Oh, they're pretty mean, all right, but just until we change the Master Ordinance."

Suddenly I wasn't liking this "we" business one little bit.

"What about the invincibility formula?" I demanded. "Why don't you make some more of that?"

Dr. Freedelhum sighed. "I don't think that

was one of our better ideas," he admitted.

Jamie looked glum. "I thought of all the people on Kerbosky and how they might never be free again. I just wanted to help. I knew we'd have to be really strong to go up against four billion robots. It was my idea about the invincible part, but I didn't think it through. It needed some very special ingredients not available on Earth, ones that couldn't be created in the automatic molecular transformer."

Dr. Freedelhum whispered into the computer again and a video appeared on the screen. It showed hundreds of sad-eyed people marching and bowing. They were carrying objects and putting them down. The sound track was just a lot of groans and moans.

"They've all been crying," I said. "Look at their eyes. They're totally red."

"They probably all have been crying," Jamie admitted, "but that's not why their eyes are red."

"Huh?" I asked.

Jamie nodded. "All Kerboskians have red or purple eyes."

"But you don't . . . " I started to say when Jamie passed his hand across his eyes. When

I could see his face again, something had changed. It was as if all his features had altered just slightly. Sure, he still had a nose and a mouth, but they looked a little askew. It was his eyes that caught my attention, though. They were a brilliant red and seemed to bore into my own. When Dr. Freedelhum removed his pince-nez, his eyes were a deep magenta shade, like the kind in the crayon box.

A shiver of fear raced up my monster spine and lodged behind my molars. Jamie had looked so ordinary when he had been in my class. No one would have looked at him twice. He'd been in the common nerd category, the same as me, at least until he came up with that "I'm an alien" story. Now he had abruptly moved into the definitely strange department. His eyes were giving me the willies. Then again, I wasn't any better. I had enough scales and fangs and beady red eyes and excess drool to make whole schoolyards of kids scream Yuck.

Dr. Freedelhum replaced his pince-nez on his long nose, and his eyes became more human. I brushed the drool away with my claw. Jamie passed his hand over his eyes again and they turned brown. "Didn't want to scare anyone on Earth," he said, "so we got these neat contact lenses and used electromagnetism to rearrange our molecules ever so slightly."

I stared, maw open, purple tongue flicking in and out. "I think I need to go home now," I said.

Dr. Freedelhum pressed fast-forward on the computer video and the Kerboskian citizens performed Herculean labors in quick time. Flashes of silver zipped across the screen and the citizens bowed again and again as if they were doing their exercises.

"The robots," Jamie whispered, like he hadn't heard me at all. "All Kerboskians will have to do the will of the robots for ever and ever. We can't let that happen. Everyone I've ever known is a slave."

Dr. Freedelhum smiled thoughtfully. "I've got a much better plan than the invincibility formula," he said. "I know how the robots can be defeated." He grinned at me through his pince-nez and I knew right away that I wasn't going to like this plan one bit. "You see, Campy, the robots have a giant zoo. They are making a collection of all the species in the known universe. You know, to study them."

"To make it easier to enslave them?" I asked.

Dr. Freedelhum clapped me on the scales. "You're a quick learner!" he said. "The rest will be no problem for you."

"The rest?" My tail was lashing around, making Jamie and Dr. Freedelhum duck and cover under the computer console. The thrashing tail was a nervous habit, I discovered, of Campythronagithicus Fabutali.

"Of course they will find you sooo interesting, being a mythological creature. They will want to find out exactly what makes you tick and if all those stories about your strange powers are true or not. They will want to experiment on you piece by piece . . ."

"Hold it right there," I snarled. "First, I don't have any powers, strange or not, and second, if I get it, you are going to give me to the robots to experiment on and — "

"Only briefly. By then you'll be into the Nerve Center and, presto."

There was that word again. I was liking this whole idea less and less. Me. Robbie Packford, the monster, up against billions of robots who had no idea what being nice meant, who wanted to do evil experiments on my monster body and brain.

"No!" I croaked. "No, no, no! I am not going to be part of this crazy plan. You two must be nuts. Why don't the pair of you turn yourselves into alien monsters and zip back down to your home planet? Nosh down two billion robots each. That would just about solve your problem!"

Dr. Freedelhum looked a little surprised. "You don't have to get so emotional about it," he said flatly, polishing his pince-nez on the sleeve of his white scientist's coat until they gleamed in the reflections from the blinking computer lights. "Besides, you have the perfect bio-signature to confuse the robots."

"Duhhh," I growled with monster intelligence.

Dr. Freedelhum hadn't stopped cleaning his pince-nez. He wasn't even looking at me. I felt like crunching those ridiculous glasses into a mangled mess with one swipe of my claws. "The planet is shielded. The information was in the last transmission. If Jamie or I were to attempt to transport down, our Kerboskian bio-signatures would be recognized and . . . " Dr. Freedelhum shook his curly head sadly and replaced his sparkling pince-nez on the end of his nose. He stared at me over their tops. "Immediate incarceration," he added. "No possibility of us reaching the Nerve Center. But you can, Campy. You are the final plan. They will never suspect that an entity as strange as you is the secret agent intent on changing the Master Ordinance."

Jamie took my claw in his hand and looked straight into my beady red eyes. "Do you have a better plan?" he asked.

I gulped. I was stumped. I hadn't had a plan since we made the toothpick bridge in science project at school and mine fell down because I got too elaborate. I shook my head and my scales rattled.

"You have to help us, Robbie." Jamie's vision was still locked onto mine. Brown eyes to beady red ones. "Think of the enslaved Kerboskians longing for freedom. Without your help, it's all over — Kerbosky, the whole universe, everything."

I sighed again, hot breath pouring from

my large nostrils. Dr. Freedelhum had ordered the computer to show a still photo, Kerboskians with red-rimmed eyes, gazing hopelessly into the camera's eye like they'd just lost their last friend in the universe. I mean, with a question like that, what's a monster to do?

Chapter Five

First one eye popped open. Then the other. I began to scream and I kept on screaming. I was in space. Stars and planets hurtled by me. A black hole opened up to my right. Streams of light zoomed into it and disappeared, gobbled up. I was next; I knew it. The end, I thought.

A light snapped on and a voice shouted my name. "Robbie, Robbie, what's the matter?"

My head swung around. In front of the streaming stars was Jamie. "Jamie," I gasped, "the black hole, it's pulling me in!"

Jamie rushed over. "Robbie, it's just a nightmare. You're okay."

"But it's still happening," I growled. "Can't you see it? A giant red planet just about decimated us. Look out! That was close. An asteroid as big as a mountain. Whew, at least we're still in one piece." I buried my head in my claws.

Jamie put his arm around me. Then he was shaking me. "Did you take the Glicko Goo? You were supposed to take some before we went into space drive. Don't you remember?"

My red beady eyes traveled to the cream-colored platform beside my bed through which planets seemed to be hurtling. The goo was still there, sticky as ever.

Jamie was still shaking me. "Don't you see, Robbie?" he exclaimed. "You're seeing through the hull of the spaceship. You do have strange powers."

It was true. When I shook my head, Jamie solidified in front of me and I could see him in the space cabin where I had gone to bed before the space jump back to his home galaxy. When I closed my eyes and opened them I could see the stars and planets again, red dwarfs, asteroids, suns.

Jamie was pulling me out of bed. "See if you can do the rest of the things," he demanded.

"What?"

"Like we read on the computer. Make yourself fly. I know you can do it!"

I shrugged my armored shoulders and rubbed my scales against the cupboard. Then I climbed up on the bed and jumped off. I crashed to the floor with a resounding thud. "I don't think they got the flying part quite right," I said, rubbing my elbow with my claws. No broken scales. I probably could have become a human — I mean monster — battering ram without so much as a dent or a scratch.

"Think light," suggested Jamie. "Think like a bird."

I imagined myself on a diet, getting lighter and lighter. I imagined myself a bird with hollow bones. I thought about what a bird's eye view of the Earth would look like, with me a speck in the air high off the surface.

"It's working. It's working," Jamie screamed.

My eyes popped open. My monster body was hovering about two feet off the ground. When I moved my tail, it was like a rudder. My claws were like a conductor's hands, conducting the music of my flight. I floated around the room and began to giggle. I made myself zoom around the space cabin, making Jamie duck and squeal, "Watch out, Robbie! You barely missed me." I looked down from the rounded dome of the ceiling and took in the amazing bed that Jamie had explained could make itself and tuck itself away into the wall. In the corner was the round window of the automatic molecular processor that could produce enough junk food to drown a galaxy in the blink of an eye. This was really fun.

When I closed and opened my eyes, I could see Dr. Freedelhum in the next space cabin. He was snoring in his bed and had forgotten to take off his pince-nez. Each time he snored they wiggled on the end of his nose. His arm was stretched across the top of the sheets. His pajamas had green frogs and yellow duckies on them. I was beginning to think that Jamie could be a real friend because he didn't seem like a nerd anymore. But Dr. Freedelhum? Well, he still seemed pretty strange to me, and the PJs didn't help. If they were another example of Dr. Freedelhum's Earth research, I hoped he'd never change jobs and become a fashion consultant.

Jamie interrupted my flight. "Be invisible now, Robbie. You can do it. That will cinch it with the robots."

How to be invisible? If thinking light made me float and fly, what should I think about to be invisible? I closed my eyes, imagining myself on a dark night out in the country with no moon or stars. No one could see me, not even the night creatures. In my imagination I was fading out. I was becoming the night itself, no more than a soft breeze in the black sky.

"It's working," Jamie called again. "You're fading in and out. I can't see you at all, just a tiny shadow. How'd you do that?"

Now I was really giggling. I could make myself turn visible and invisible. It was like turning a light on or off. I could look at the room or see stars shooting off in a million directions in space. I could float up till my head bumped against the ceiling or stay standing on solid ground.

I looked down at Jamie from the ceiling. He was looking better and better to me, better and better to eat. I floated down towards him, my huge tongue rolling across my fangs, swooping up the globs of saliva that dribbled down my scaly chin.

"Robbie!" Jamie cried out in alarm. "I don't like the way you're looking at me."

I snapped back to myself. "The goo," I growled. "You'd better give it to me if you don't want to be my breakfast."

Jamie grabbed the sticky mess off the platform and tossed it into my open maw. It squirted against the back of my throat. Each time it tasted different, but good. I swallowed it in one gulp, and before I had a chance to burp I thudded down to the floor.

"Hey," I cried out, "I can't fly anymore or see through the walls or become invisible."

"The goo," said Jamie.

"Huh?"

"If you eat the Glicko Goo you can still be Robbie inside Campy's body, but you can't do all the monster tricks."

My monster brain could hardly take in what Jamie was saying. Great, I thought. I had two choices. I could be this Robbie monster who couldn't do anything and who was going to be locked up in some robot zoo and maybe dissected, or I could not eat the goo and do all these great tricks like flying, becoming invisible or having x-ray vision. But then there was this other problem. The powerful monster me would chow down on my only two friends on this side of the universe as soon as look at them. What a dilemma!

Chapter Six

"Yes, my friend, it is a dilemma," mused Dr. Freedelhum, looking at me and then shining his pince-nez thoughtfully. Luckily, he had exchanged the pajamas with the frogs and the duckies for his starched white lab coat. "But as a scientific problem it's simple, a matter of fine-tuning, if you will. Hmm. The right amount of Glicko Goo to allow you to use your powers, but not so little that you begin noshing on the first sentient being that comes your way. Yes, Plan Anti-enslavement is evolving nicely. Thinking on the run, as they say."

I wasn't sure that I liked Dr. Freedelhum's definition of my dilemma. "If you don't get it right," I said, "just about anybody could be down the hatch for breakfast. It wouldn't be my fault. I wouldn't be able to help it."

Dr. Freedelhum nodded. "Just your Campy self coming out. Of course, there is the other danger — "

"Danger," I squeaked. If I had hair it would have been standing on end. As it was, my tail lashed around violently instead.

Dr. Freedelhum rolled his chair closer to my snout. "You need those powers to get to the Nerve Center to change the Master Ordinance, but you need your human self to know what to do with the computer. Ancient mythological creatures may have strange and amazing powers, but they just aren't up on computers. You will need some of the Glicko Goo, but, of course, if you don't take any for awhile, it's not only the eating up of other creatures that is bothersome."

Bothersome! That was Dr. Freedelhum's word for it. Talk about understatement.

"You see, my boy, there is always the possibility that without the Glicko Goo, Robbie Packford as we have known him will cease to exist."

"What!" I shrieked.

"Yes," continued Dr. Freedelhum, "you

were pretty far gone when we discovered you in the alley. A few hours more and who knows — "

"You mean, poof or, presto, or whatever it is, I would just be a people-eating monster?" Not even purple, I thought.

Jamie patted my claw. "But we did get there in time, Robbie, and you are still you."

"But look at me," I wailed. "I don't want to look like this. I don't want to have to be careful I don't chomp through my tongue whenever I eat or think of my little sister as a snack for the rest of my life."

"We can get you back to normal. I promise, cross my heart and hope to die, just like they say on earth," Jamie pledged, making a crossed sign over where his heart area would have been if he were human. But then, who knew exactly where Kerboskians kept their hearts? "Just as soon as we figure out the problem with the robots and the Nerve Center. They're really nice robots. They'd do anything for you. It's the Master Ordinance. As soon as you change it back to BE NICE — "

"Hold it," I yelped. "First, what's this promise part? I don't remember you being so great with the invincibility formula, and what is the Master Ordinance for these really nice robots right now and how did it get changed anyway?" I was missing some important facts here.

Dr. Freedelhum smiled, but it wasn't the kind of smile that made you feel good. Maybe cats smiled at mice that way. Maybe monsters like me smiled at their victims that way just before they noshed down on them.

"Er," he said at last. "It was kind of a mistake."

Kind of a mistake. This wasn't like making a mistake in long division. It wasn't even like forgetting to do your weekend chores. This little mistake was about to enslave the universe. A horrible suspicion formed in my mind. I looked back and forth between the only two unenslaved Kerboskians. I stared until a bit of a blush crept across Dr. Freedelhum's face.

Shivers ran up and down my scales. "I can guess who made the mistake," I said.

"Dear boy," began Dr. Freedelhum, "it was such an innocent, tiny sort of error. Who would have thought?"

Now I knew the truth. I was locked up on a spaceship with a couple of loonies who had just let billions of crazed robots enslave their own planet, robots that were now poised to take on the rest of the universe.

"Uh-uh," I said. "I am not going to be part of this crazy scheme."

"But."

"No."

"Aw, come on."

"No."

"Pretty please."

"No, no, no, and no sugar on top either."

Chapter Seven

"Let's go over things one more time, Robbie," said Jamie.

We'd been over it a million times already. I'd have to have been brain dead to forget. But that wasn't the worst part. Far worse was the thought that I was now just as crazy as that pair from Kerbosky, Jamie and Dr. Freedelhum. I was one monster-hop from the teleporter. They were going to beam me down to the planet Kerbosky, where billions of not-nice robots were waiting for me, itching to do gross things to my monster self. How had I ever said yes to this? Even though my words had said, "No, no, no," when Jamie looked at me with his pleading brown eyes (or were they red?) what choice did I have?

My monster brain ached.

"Glicko Goo," said Jamie.

"Check," I said, patting a scale on my neck. Not actually a scale, but a pouch that looked exactly like a scale, which Jamie had made in the molecular processor. In it were a week's supply of miniaturized Glicko Goo pills. Just one a day, they had warned. Keep the balance between having monster powers and still having Robbie Packford's thoughts at the back of your brain. The pill was timed-release, but they hadn't had time to perfect it. It worked pretty quickly, but when I first took it my powers would disappear for a bit, and as the pill wore off, well, everyone already knew that part. Everything that moved started looking good to eat.

"Universal translator."

"Check," I said, touching where my human ear should have been. I had to give Jamie and Dr. Freedelhum credit. They had disguised the little gold ring and colored it a greeny brown to fit in with my scales. Now I just looked like any old mythological creature conjured up from dim eons past.

"Communication device."

"Check." I touched my right claw to my snout, where a teeny-tiny communicator had been implanted so I could talk with Dr. Freedelhum and Jamie back at the spaceship. They could direct me and give the instructions about how to change the Master Ordinance in the Nerve Center of the main computer.

"You want a snack from the molecular food processor before you go?" asked Jamie.

I shook my head. It sounded too much like a prisoner's last meal before . . . Don't even think about it, I warned myself.

"You are going to be a great success," exclaimed Dr. Freedelhum, clapping me on my back scales. "You will be a hero after this and a scientific curiosity as well."

Jamie shook my claw solemnly. "You will be a hero, Robbie. Maybe you'll even get the Kerbosky Medal of Honor. You're going to save our planet."

"And the universe," chimed in Dr. Freedelhum, edging me towards the teleporter. Before I could scream, "I don't really want to do this" or "It's all a mistake," the sapphire blue light enveloped me. My molecules wavered and shimmered. I didn't want to be a hero. I didn't want the Kerbosky Medal of Honor. I wished I had never met Jamie and Dr. Freedelhum. I . . .

Chapter Eight

I suppose, as planets go, it was probably fine, but it also was — well — different. For instance, let's start with the vegetation. I never knew how much I liked green until I got a gander of the red stuff that grew on Kerbosky. A million shades of it. Tall plumy trees with feathers growing out of them and scaly brown-red bark. Blood-red flowers with magenta leaves. Thorny bushes with round scarlet leaves and little plants that looked like orange sausages. I wondered how much of the vegetation of Kerbosky was poisonous. Dr. Freedelhum and Jamie had forgotten to give me any information about the Kerboskian equivalent of, say, poison ivy or stinging nettles. I stood on the red grass and looked around. The monster claws on my monster toes made deep indentations in the red carpet of grass. I let out a long monster sigh. Was I supposed to go looking for the robots or would they just find me? And how long would it take them to start being not nice to me?

I plodded through the red grass past the flame-like plumes of trees, dragging my tail behind me unhappily. "Testing, testing," I whispered. "I'm here. Come in, Jamie and Dr. Freedelhum."

My snout buzzed and I squinched it up, trying not to sneeze. Then a voice whispered from inside my snout, "Great, Robbie, just find the main road and head towards Robotica. That's the robot city. It used to be the capital of Kerbosky, but now the robots have taken it over and put most of the people in jail — that is, the ones who aren't waiting hand and foot on the robots. When you see the robots, don't run away. They won't like that."

"What do they like?" I asked.

"They used to like getting their joints oiled," Jamie said, "and fetching things for Kerboskians."

"What about now?" I asked.

"Now, I don't think they like anything

much, except enslaving others. They want all other species to serve them. Just do whatever they say and smile."

I tried to make my jaws move into a smile and felt a drop of saliva run down my front fang. Campy smiling might just be out. Better to keep my mouth closed. Not-nice robots probably weren't too keen on fangs, and I didn't want to look hostile.

I looked around again, stepping over the blood-red flowers. There was no road in sight, only red hills, red trees, red everything under a yellow sky that could turn your stomach. Maybe Jamie and Dr. Freedelhum felt the same way about Earth, but I couldn't imagine myself getting used to this color scheme. One direction looked as good as another. Red grass grew everywhere, dotted with the deeper red of flowers and occasional feathery trees.

I squinted and stared through the yellow haze. I could just make out the sun, no, two suns, hanging in the sky, one moving towards one horizon and one towards the other. Back on the spaceship, Jamie had tried to explain how the orbits worked. There was a big sun and a little one. Kerbosky orbited around the little sun and it in turn orbited around the big sun. Ellipses within ellipses. The mathematical part of my brain wondered about the gravitational pull between the suns and how it might affect the planet, but my monster self couldn't take it all in. I patted the Glicko Goo pouch. It had been awhile since I had taken a pill. Might as well find out now if my monster powers still worked. Otherwise, it was game over.

I squeezed my beady red eyes shut and imagined myself getting lighter and lighter, like one of the red 'feather-like' leaves on the trees. When I opened my eyes I was floating about two feet from the ground. I gave my body instructions with my brain to make myself go up and down, just like Jamie had me practice back on the spaceship. "You may not be perfect," he had said, "but you have to know how to maneuver."

I wished I could fly way up into the yellow sky and look down on the countryside, but that would be too dangerous. Who knew when the robots would come marching by with their computerized brains stuck in attack mode? I made myself go invisible a few times and I practiced looking right through the red plume trees, but all I saw were more of the same on the other side.

A red dragonfly-like insect buzzed lazily by. It hovered over the top of my head as if thinking about what to do next. This beauty was about sixteen times the size of an average mosquito. I hoped it didn't sting. It made me remember the T-shirt Aunt Rose had brought back from Manitoba with the picture of a giant mosquito on it. The caption read, "I gave blood in Winnipeg." The insect buzzed angrily and dive-bombed. Before I could duck, it zapped into a scale on my forehead. Nothing happened. The insect wobbled away on shaky red wings.

I was invincible! Nothing could get through these armored scales.

I trudged on through the redness and began to think that some of the flowers matched the color of my eyes. I hummed songs in my mind to keep on going. I had been so worried and now my great adventure was getting boring!

Finally I sat down under one of the giant red plume trees, careful to find the only bit of shade available when two suns were shining down from the sky. I hadn't heard from Jamie and Dr. Freedelhum for a while, but that didn't bother me. They had said that when the spaceship went around the other side of the planet, communication would get a little fuzzy. It also had something to do with the vibrations the communicator caused inside my snout, but I couldn't exactly remember that part. Right, I said to myself, they've probably ordered up some great fast food from the molecular food processor while I'm stuck here, tired and hungry. They were probably having a bit of a snooze while I buzzed them on my snout communicator until I started to sneeze and mowed down a few plants. One thing you really don't want to do is make a Campythronagithicus Fabutali sneeze.

"Sorry," I said to no one in particular. Falling asleep was not a good idea, but this bit of shade felt pretty good. I would close my eyes for one minute, just one. Dr. Freedelhum's image danced in my brain, snoring while his pince-nez wiggled up and down on the end of his nose, his body decorated with row upon row of green frogs and yellow duckies.

The ducks began to open their orange beaks. Their bright yellow faded to the same bilious color as the Kerboskian air. They began to march around and around like a parade. Then the frogs joined them, jumping off scarlet lily pads. Their little eyes were blinding flashes of red light. The frogs glowed pinkly, as if someone had turned on a red light behind them. All that color started to hurt my brain.

The ducks quacked, quietly at first and then louder and louder. The pink frogs loomed over me, their mouths growing. I put my hands over my ears to stop their awful croaking. Then I turned cold. I opened one of my beady eyes.

A grating voice was speaking to me, drowning out the quacking and the croaking, but, believe me, I'd rather hear the frogs and duckies any time, no matter what color they were.

"Do not move, sentient being," grated a monotonous voice. "An atomic vaporizer is pointed at your brain or where your brain is predicted to be by my computer banks. One false move and your atoms will be scattered across the universe."

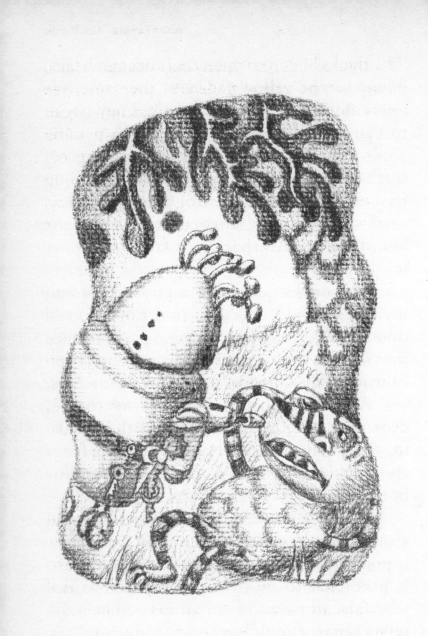

I gulped. A gray machine with some kind of weapon pointing at me was hovering over my body. I knew I should have thought about this part. In the movies the hero always has some great line right at this point. He shows he's brave and funny all at once. But my brain was stuck in neutral. I stared down the end of the silver weapon. Seconds separated me from atomic vaporization.

Maybe it wasn't my choice to be a Campythronagithicus Fabutali, but I was getting used to my monster body, even kind of fond of it, and didn't want its atoms all around the universe. I wondered what the mathematical chances were of getting all those atoms back together in the right order, once the metal finger of the robot had pushed the button of the atomic vaporizer.

"Ummmm," I said at last, my great line, as I continued to stare at the gray machine.

It had a computer screen for a face and six little antenna stalks on its head with yellow eyes stuck on top of them, probably so it could look forwards and backwards and sideways all at once. It had two arms and a utility belt that would have made Batman jealous.

I didn't want to know how any of those gadgets worked. They all looked sharp and mean. It had two sets of wheels, but right now it was hovering off the ground about a foot in the air.

Jamie and Dr. Freedelhum had probably forgotten to tell me that all the amazing powers I possessed were just normal for robots. Its computer face squinted at me and the eyestalks regarded me: the first two, then the second two and finally the third two, intertwining themselves around each other. I felt like they were boring holes right through my scales.

"Identify yourself, sentient being. You do not compute."

"I'm a Campythronagithicus Fabutali," I croaked.

"Do not move," ordered the gravelly monotone voice. "I must check my computer banks . . . Not found," said the robot after a few seconds of blinking and whirring.

"I'm a mythological creature," I offered, attempting to smile, feeling wet saliva dripping down my fangs and onto my scales.

The robot snorted, or at least that's what it sounded like. "Robots deal only with facts," it said. "Myth is untrue. It does not compute."

Again the machine blinked and whirred. I considered. One, leaping up and grabbing the weapon like they do in the movies. The good guy NEVER gets shot. Two, becoming invisible. Three, begging for mercy. Four — before I got to four the machine had computed something or other.

"Interesting specimen, not found in memory banks," it said. "Must investigate and report. Do not move."

I tried to look as friendly as a monster could. A minute or two later I felt a rush of wind above me, and a silver ship landed nearby without a sound. It was a shiny smooth disc, regular issue for any science fiction movie. A hatch opened and two more identical robots rolled out. When they saw me they began to levitate and blink and whir.

"Interesting specimen," they said at last. "Get in space cruiser. Walk slowly. Keep limbs by side."

"Where are we going?" I growled, finally finding my voice. But the robots carried on, ignoring me.

"Interesting specimen," they repeated, "not in computer banks." Then I heard the fateful words. "Take specimen to laboratory."

I thought about using my powers to levitate into the yellow sky, but the door of the space cruiser had already closed. I was trapped inside with the three robots. Their atomic vaporizers were still trained on me. They fiddled with a control panel and the ship lifted into the air.

I huddled in the corner. My snout buzzed and I heard a whisper. It was Dr. Freedelhum. "Our plan is going just right," he said. "Soon you will escape and find the Nerve Center and change the Master Ordinance."

It was easy for him to talk like that. He was safe in orbit around Kerbosky with yummy snacks available night and day. No one was going to experiment on his body. No one was threatening to blast his atoms around the universe.

I wanted my atoms just the way they were and I wanted to go home. But the silent space cruiser moved swiftly forward, and when I craned my monster neck and stared with my beady red eyes out the spaceport, I saw a city rushing towards me with dazzling speed, great domes and towers. It stood out starkly against the yellow sky and the red vegetation. The city of the robots was as black as night.

Chapter Nine

The cell where the robots put me was clean and dry. I had been imagining a moldy dungeon with a pallet of straw and one tiny barred window that hardly let in any light. But everything here at the Robot Scientific Research Center was new and up-to-date. In fact, everything gleamed metallically at me. The only thing I wasn't certain about was the company. My cell was already occupied by several odd creatures who regarded me suspiciously. A purple one with horns snorted. Another troll-like one looked at me balefully with yellow eyes. The last, an overgrown hamster type with hair everywhere, whimpered in the corner.

I parted my leathery lips and smiled. That made the hairy one whimper all the more, so I snapped my jaws shut before any saliva oozed out. I stared at the other creatures It was more like a cage in a high-tech SPCA than a dungeon. I thought of mad scientists and animal experimentation and would have broken out into a cold sweat if monster bodies could sweat. The other creatures huddled away from me. Probably I didn't have anything to fear from them. They were as terrified as I was. "Hey," I said, rubbing my universal translator with my claw. "I'm friendly. When do we eat around here?"

I was greeted by a series of whimpers, squeaks and growls. Luckily, the universal translator was doing its job just fine and I heard their questions right inside my head, clear as day.

"Who are you?"

"P-p-please don't hurt us."

"How did you get here?"

"What are those shiny creatures going to do to us?"

"The food is terrible."

I wasn't going to get any useful information from the quivering mass of flesh in front of me. They may have looked like creatures out of some scary movie, except for the hamster, but they wouldn't hurt a fly.

I asked my own questions anyhow.

"How many robots control this place? Do they all have weapons? Have any creatures had their atoms blasted into space? Have you seen the Nerve Center? How do I get there? And exactly how 'not nice' are these robots anyhow?"

The creature assortment replied, "Uhh, duh, don't know," and "P-p-p-please don't eat me."

Some help you guys are, I thought. It was up to me and my partners back on the spaceship.

"Come in, Jamie and Dr. Freedelhum," I buzzed quietly through my snout.

Jamie sounded far away, as if we were on a bad connection. "Where are you, Robbie?"

"In robot jail," I replied, "with a purple dragon, a troll and a hamster who looks like a fur explosion that won't quit whimpering."

Dr. Freedelhum's voice broke in. "Good start, my boy. Now just get to the Nerve Center and — "

"Presto," I finished for him.

"Exactly," continued the doctor. "You just have to time it right. You have to be enough of Robbie to understand our instructions and modify the computer program, but enough of Campy to do a little fast disappearing."

I groaned.

"How long since you took your last miniaturized Glicko Goo pill?" he demanded.

I checked my wrist where my glow-in-the-dark digital watch should have been. Of course, now I only had green-brown scales. "Awhile," I answered.

"Don't take the Glicko right now," whispered Dr. Freedelhum. "Become invisible when the robots feed you or take you out for — er — experimentation."

I didn't like the sound of that word and began to think I'd watched too many horror movies in my short life. An image of Frankenstein slunk up from my brain stem and lodged in my visual cortex. As I listened, my beady eyes roved the cell and outside the bars to the gleaming metallic room. Idly, I glanced at the shivering ball of hamster hair groaning in the corner.

My eyes fastened on its haunches, plump,

cute hamster haunches. Yummy, delicious hamster haunches. Food, said my Campy brain, fresh meat. I began to salivate. A cold shiver raced down my spine and a sinking feeling grew in my empty stomach. This just wasn't going to work.

In the meantime, Dr. Freedelhum's words buzzed on in my nostril. The last thing I heard him say was "Presto" before Jamie said, "Over and out."

I sneezed a small sneeze as the buzzing in my snout stopped, but even small monster sneezes are pretty loud. The hamster shook like a hairy bowl of jelly. Even when he was shaking as if he had been trapped on an arctic ice floe, he looked tastier and tastier. My long tongue slurped across my razor-sharp fangs. My spiked tail lashed. I took one baby step towards the shivering fur ball, then another. Soon I was looming over the creature.

"P-p-p-please," it wailed. "I promise I don't taste good. I may look succulent, but you see it's all hair. Underneath, I'm skin and bone. You wouldn't enjoy me at all."

I could smell the compelling odor of the

miserable little creature with my keen monster nose. Fresh meat. Kill. My great monster jaws opened. Saliva poured from my red throat. My beady eyes focused in on the kill.

Chapter Ten

A grating metallic voice broke my Campy concentration. My gaping jaws, about to be buried in hamster haunch, turned towards the sound.

"Food," grated the robot, "food, for sentient creatures before experimentation."

The last bit of Robbie Packford's consciousness stared through the greedy beady eyes of the Campythronagithicus Fabutali. The robot unlocked the cage door with a sensor. Another behind him aimed an atomic vaporizer at our heads. Two more pushed a trough of steaming, evil-smelling food through the open door. Their intertwining eyestalks twitched.

The robots appeared to be talking to themselves. "Experiment," they said to each other. If robots could be said to look happy, these ones seemed pretty cheerful. "Plans for conquering the universe almost complete."

"We will be masters of all," added the one with the atomic vaporizer.

"Never take orders again," said the one with the door sensor. Its computer-screen face seemed to smile as its eyestalks glanced at the robots behind it.

Now or never, I thought as the robots stirred the sticky orange mess in the trough with a long metal spoon. Robbie, don't leave me now, I said to myself. I don't want to be a monster. It was time to use my talents. It was time to disappear.

I imagined myself fading out gradually. I didn't want to give anyone a shock. The troll and the purple dragon couldn't care less. All they cared about was their next meal, which might well be their last. The hamster continued to whimper and shake, luckily distracting the robots. They prodded him with their metallic fingers.

"This one only skin and bones," said one of the robots. "Too much hair. Sentient creatures should eat nourishment provided by robots."

"You see," squeaked the hamster, "it's true. I'm not good to eat."

Now I was totally invisible. Hardly daring to breathe, I made my monster feet and claws pad quickly past the guards. My great purple tongue gathered only one slurp of the evil-smelling food in the trough. Not half as good as fresh hamster meat, but it had to do for now.

One of the robots looked around. "Four sentient creatures?" it questioned. "Now only three."

They looked puzzled even for robots, and masses of equations flashed across their computer-screen faces, but I was already out of the cell and padding quickly (with only a few scratching noises made by my claws on the metallic floor) down the hall. The Nerve Center, I thought, must get to it. Food, said the other part of my brain insistently, fresh meat, kill. I passed an assortment of aliens in the other cells that *Star Wars* would have been proud of. In my state of mind, they all looked good to eat, even the pudgy wormy wrinkled one with seven waving green antennae springing from its mud brown skin.

When I got around the corner I buzzed through my snout in a panic. "The Nerve Center," I whispered hoarsely, "which direction?" Metallic tunnels led off in all directions, gleaming silver in the glare from recessed lights in the ceiling. I'd never find it. Maybe I should just give up and nosh down on a few sentient beings.

"Keep to the right, always to the right," Dr. Freedelhum's voice buzzed in my snout. He didn't sound too confident. I was sure he was guessing, but what the heck. I bore right. Suddenly the tunnel was filled with robots whirring and rolling on their tiny wheels. Their eyestalks looked forwards and backwards and sideways all at the same time. Think light, I ordered myself. My monster body floated above them until I rested against the smooth ceiling of the tunnel. On and on they passed below me, ten in a row, row upon row. I counted the rows for a while, but soon it was too much for my monster brain. There must have been a thousand or more.

Snatches of robot conversation reached my monster brain through the universal translator. "Expeditionary force. Conquer all known worlds. Milky Way, next target. All sentient planets to come under our control. Robots will be served. They will no longer serve. The universe is ours."

It went on and on until my brain hurt, but the worst part was that this army was only the tiniest bit of the whole robot army. Millions of groups like this were whirring down other corridors on the way to waiting spaceships. The robots were poised to take over the universe. It was now or never for the Nerve Center.

I floated through corridor after corridor over armies of robots, my mind alternating between the horror of robot takeover and the desire for fresh meat. My Robbie self struggled to remain conscious, but my monster self was growing stronger and stronger. If I took the miniaturized Glicko Goo pill before I found the Nerve Center, I was finished. A billion robots with atomic vaporizers would be all over me.

I began to do the times tables in my mind to keep on being Robbie. I went through the scoring stats for the National Hockey League, though I'd missed a lot of games. Who knows, it was probably close to the play-offs by now. I even tried to work out the chances of what was happening to me actually happening. Those odds were uncomputable by humans. No one would believe this. I didn't believe it myself.

Below me the armies of robots whirred towards the destruction of whole planets and, boy, were they in a bad mood. I could not imagine them being nice to anybody.

Faster and faster I floated, doing the only thing I could. Bear right, bear right. When the seemingly endless corridors parted, I followed Dr. Freedelhum's single instruction. Now I was whizzing above the robots. They had become a gray blur below me. How long did I have before those waiting spacecraft were launched and the robot war began? I imagined my own little planet, the shining blue ball of Earth, cradled in an outer arm of the Milky Way, unsuspecting of doom until . . .

Crash! I thudded against a steel door. My claws scraped the bright metal as I slid to the ground. Beyond me the robots droned, intent on conquest. They didn't notice the few scratches in the steel made by my monster claws. They didn't hear the thud of my body or even my loud "ouch." They only had one thought in their computer consoles and that was to conquer the universe. They whirred towards the completion of their task.

What could I do now? My way was blocked by a solid steel door. I huddled, dazed, on the cold metal floor, thinking that monster headaches were something you didn't want to write home about. Slowly, my beady red eyes refocused. My monster self felt only hunger, intense hunger. Visions of fresh meat danced through my brain, furry hamsters, scrawny or not under all that hair, plump little human sisters, even Jamie and Dr. Freedelhum.

Then my beady red eyes opened wide and stared. Suddenly I was looking through the metal of the door. Inside, in a bright room, shinier and larger than all the countless corridors I had passed through, sat a giant computer. Panels and lights flashed everywhere. Robot workers craned their eyestalks and talked in monotone computer language. A thousand screens flashed with information. The Robot Nerve Center. I had found it!

Chapter Eleven

Just as I was wondering how I'd ever get in there, a panel opened soundlessly in the door and two robots appeared behind me, their eyestalks twitching. Just in time I floated off the ground and up above their heads. As they rolled through the door, I took a deep breath and floated invisibly after them.

It was just as well that Campythronagithicus Fabutalis didn't have metal on their menu because those robots would have been goners. My human self was a bare flicker of consciousness in the back of my reptilian brain. The Robbie part of me said, Go into the Nerve Center. The monster part thought only of food, fresh meat, kill. It was getting harder and harder for me — the Robbie Packford part, that is — to think. My snout buzzed with instructions that my reptilian brain could hardly process.

Once I was in place at the computer screens, I had to take a Glicko Goo pill so that I could understand what Dr. Freedelhum was telling me. But then my powers would wear off and I'd be visible to the robots. Some of them had atomic vaporizers in their utility belts. Not one of them looked even a bit nice. I was sorry I'd left that shaking, whimpering hamster behind down those many long corridors. I'd have done anything for one bite of its juicy haunch right now, hair and all.

Dismally, I floated above the computer screen and the robots. They were planning the final attack launching of the spaceships, an armada of thousands and thousands of ships heading into their own galaxy and beyond. The numbers made my brain hurt. Master Ordinance, I kept repeating to myself, Master Ordinance. Then I saw a tiny movement of yellow in the corner. My beady red eyes opened wide and saliva dripped from my fangs. A furry mouse-like creature with two tails and an explosion of whiskers had shot out from under a chair. It froze momentarily in the bright lights of the Nerve Center. How could that succulent-looking creature have made it through all those shiny steel walls? I didn't care. It was only a mouthful, but one juicy morsel was better than nothing. I hovered. I floated. Of course, the unsuspecting dainty morsel could not sense the invisible presence looming above it.

Inside my mind a terrible war had begun. Monster brain: Eat creature. Robbie brain: No, Master Ordinance. I put my monster claws over my eyes and groaned. One of the robots looked up. I froze.

It turned back to its computer panel and the lights flashed some more. "Ready for countdown," said the robot beneath me.

This was it, the final countdown. My Robbie part imagined my hometown overrun with robots. Campy would never eat my little sister. The robots would get her first. Who knew what they would do to her. I'd never see her skipping in front of the house with her giggling friends. I'd never get to call her names again and hear Mom and Dad's comforting voices saying to me, "Cut that out this instant, Robbie."

We've got to work together, I said to the monster brain part. You can eat later, as much as you like. You can chow down on hamsters, even on cute little bunny rabbits, just get me to the Nerve Center. Slowly, my monster body floated towards the center of the room. I was so hungry that I left a trail of saliva on the floor. The robots did not turn their heads. All their eyestalks were riveted on the flashing computer screens. Their metallic fingers pressed the keys at blinding speed.

Now I hovered near the largest computer in the room. The robots had put a large sign on it that conveniently read ROBOT NERVE CENTER. RESTRICTED AREA. The last thing they would expect was invisible company. I was grateful for that.

I shivered as I let my body sink to the ground. It was time to swallow the Glicko Goo. All around me the robots worked feverishly. I hoped they weren't easily distracted. My clawed front paw shook as I pressed the false scale covering the bag of pills. My monster self didn't want Robbie back because Robbie occasionally liked to eat gross things like vegetables.

That's right, I whispered inside my head, Goo pill between claws. Raise slowly to mouth. My claws paused as my monster fangs opened. Eat, I said, fresh meat. Soon.

Into my open maw I popped the tiny Glicko pill. It fizzed in the back of my throat like sour lime. Good, it was down. I held my breath, hoping I hadn't waited too long. My eyes roved the computer room, watching the robots gearing up for war. If only they'd keep on concentrating on the flashing lights. My tummy rumbled. Where had that yummy-looking little morsel gone? If ever I needed a snack to help me think, it was now.

Dr. Freedelhum's instructions buzzed through my snout. The breath whooshed out of my body in relief. Dr. Freedelhum was telling me which buttons to push. He repeated the directions and slowly my right claw dropped to the console and pressed the buttons. As I watched in fascination, my claw materialized in front of my eyes, then my leathery wrist and my scaly arm. I kept pushing the keys. At last I was into the main computer bank.

A steely voice froze my blood. "Intruder alert. Intruder alert." My head swung round and my snout splatted up against the computer screen. Instantly, the buzzing inside my snout stopped in the middle of Dr. Freedelhum's final instructions. I had broken the communications device!

The robots gathered, atomic vaporizers poised to scatter my monster atoms into a billion locations in the universe. I didn't know what to do. Without Dr. Freedelhum's instructions I could not complete the sequence to finish the changes to the Master Ordinance.

Not-nice robots were all around me. They would never be nice again. First they would be not nice to me. Then they would be not nice to everyone else in the universe. I couldn't stand it!

"Arrraahhhgggg," I growled, hot breath blasting out of my jaws in a giant rush. Lights flicked on computer screens, but the robots were unfazed.

"Intruder must be neutralized," they whirred calmly. "Ready, aim . . . "

My claws scrabbled over the keys. I pressed

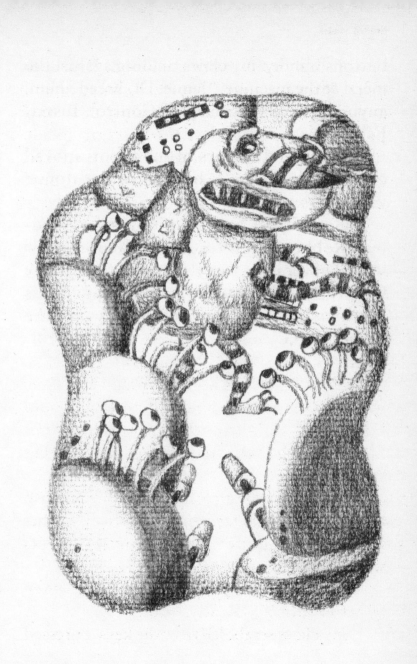

buttons blindly, my claws tinkling against the metal of the machine. "Jamie, Dr. Freedelhum, anybody, help!" I shrieked. Control. Insert. Escape.

The metal fingers of the robots moved closer to the destruct buttons of the atomic vaporizers.

Good-bye, Campy, I cried inside, Good-bye, Robbie Packford. Now I'd never grow up. I'd never even know who won the Stanley Cup for the National Hockey League this year. In less than one second I would be NOTHING.

Chapter Twelve

I held my breath and squeezed my eyes shut, trying to imagine what having your atoms scattered all over the universe felt like. It probably wasn't anything like being shot with a gun on Earth. There would be no blood, no mess to clean up, not even a little smear on the floor that used to be Robbie Packford. I waited for the end. Then nothing happened, absolutely nothing. I kept holding my monster breath until I had to gasp. I didn't want to open my eyes for fear of what my beady red eyes might see. Still nothing happened.

Then a metallic voice drone, "How may we serve you?"

My beady eyes popped open. I was still in the Robot Nerve Center standing beside the main computer. Robots were still around me, but their atomic vaporizers were no longer pointed at me. In fact, I couldn't see atomic vaporizers anywhere. And if robots could smile, which I doubted, it sure did look like these ones were smiling. They still had computer screens for faces and six twitching eyestalks, but now the twitching was different. It looked kind of, well, you know, nice.

"How may we serve you, revered sentient being?" the robot droned again.

"Identify your needs and we will do our utmost to fulfill them as swiftly as possible," said another.

"Please allow us to serve you," added a third. "That is our mission in life."

"We want to serve," they all said to me at once.

"What sort of food does the revered sentient being wish?"

"Anything you wish can be computed in the automatic molecular processor."

"May we polish your scales, revered sentient being?"

After a minute or two they were offering to floss my fangs. I couldn't stand it anymore.

I almost preferred the robots the way they had been before.

Just then a sapphire blue light lit up the corner of the Nerve Center, and out of the swirling blue appeared Jamie and Dr. Freedelhum, faintly at first and then more definite.

"Robbie," shouted Jamie, hugging my scales, "you did it. You're a hero!"

"What?" I demanded.

"Yes, my lad," Dr. Freedelhum said, "you have saved Kerbosky by reprogramming the Master Ordinance. My goodness, I think these robots are even nicer than ever."

Sure enough, the robots were trying to serve Jamie and Dr. Freedelhum, plying them with food and cushions.

Jamie grinned at me. "You see what the problem was?" he said, laughing.

I did. I remembered my grade one teacher, Mrs. Preston, saying that you couldn't be too nice. Now I knew it wasn't true. The robots were nice, sickeningly, cloyingly, disgustingly nice. I suppose because they hadn't gotten to serve anyone for a long time, all that niceness had just gotten stored up in their computer banks and they were going wild with nice.

Dr. Freedelhum glanced at the main computer. "Perhaps I could alter the Master Ordinance just slightly. Jamie, my boy, what do you think of, let's see, how about BE QUITE NICE?" The doctor tried to clean his glasses on his lab coat, but, of course, seven robots wanted to do it for him. "Or maybe BE NICE, BUT NOT TOO NICE?"

Jamie shook his head. "Dr. Freedelhum, please don't. That's how all this got started in the first place."

Dr. Freedelhum sighed. "Perhaps you are correct."

"Stop," I shouted suddenly. "What about the countdown? The millions and millions of spaceships poised to take over the universe? Billions of robots with atomic vaporizers?"

The robots looked shocked. They really did. "We are designed to serve," they grated in their monotone voices. "We never use weapons."

"But the final countdown had begun. I saw all the robots. I . . ."

Dr. Freedelhum waved his hand. "All in the past, not to worry. Things are back to normal on Kerbosky."

Jamie winked at me. "At least as normal as things can be here," he said. "But it's true about you being a hero, Robbie."

I was still confused. "How did you get here?" I growled, scratching a scale, but the robots were already scratching it for me and trying to find out if any other places on my monster body were itchy.

"When the communication device suddenly stopped working, we didn't know what had happened, so we decided the only plan of action was to teleport down here, even if it meant being instantly enslaved by the robots. We were totally out of plans."

"But when we arrived, we found you had the problem well in hand," finished Dr. Freedelhum. "And Robot 176A, I think I'd enjoy one of those Earth cappuccinos."

"Anything for you, dear doctor," whirred the machine, rushing to program the molecular processor.

The problem well in hand, I exclaimed to myself. If Dr. Freedelhum and Jamie only knew the truth. Kerbosky had been saved by blind luck. My claws must have accidentally struck the right keys. I collapsed with a thump, but the robots had anticipated my need and surrounded me with soft cushions.

"He's a hero, all right," agreed Dr. Freedelhum. "Bring the boy, I mean monster, a pizza and skip the . . ."

"Onions and olives," I finished.

"I'll have mine with everything." Dr. Freedelhum grinned. "Earth food is fascinating. I'll have to undertake a study of it, a gastronomical study, my favorite kind. Yum," he commented, biting off a big chunk. The stringy mozzarella cheese stuck to his chin.

Gratefully, and with my best monster manners, I chewed my own pizza, thinking of how, only a few minutes earlier, I had been ready to pop a two-tailed yellow rodent down my gullet. I shivered as I thought of the poor hairy hamster-like creature back in robot prison. It was time to stop being a monster and get back to being Robbie Packford. I wondered how many marks Mrs. Cardwell would dock me for being late with my socials project.

"What about getting me back to being human?" I piped up, using my long purple tongue to wipe the tomato sauce from my scaly lips.

"All in good time, Robbie," replied Dr. Freedelhum. "First you will receive the Kerboskian Medal of Honor for your bravery. It will be a great ceremony. You'll see. And . . ." Dr. Freedelhum stopped talking suddenly.

"And?"

"And we'll order pizza for everyone." All the robots clapped their metallic hands and Dr. Freedelhum gave a small bow.

Robots plumped up my cushions and asked me if there was anything more I could possibly want. I sighed. You know how, in your dreams, you imagine yourself on a holiday — sand, sun, people to serve your every whim? Somehow, all these robots with their twitching eyestalks just didn't cut it.

Chapter Thirteen

Dr. Freedelhum was as good as his word. In front of all the dignitaries of the planet Kerbosky, and with countless robots whirring and floating and interrupting every two seconds with offers of food and backrubs, I received my Kerbosky Medal of Honor from the president. He was a little man, about my size but with tufty gray hair springing out of his ears and a round little belly that stuck out over his belt. Instead of a starched white lab coat like Dr. Freedelhum, he wore the official uniform of Kerbosky, a blood-red suit with brass buttons and epaulettes and a plumed red hat that resembled the feathery tree I had fallen asleep under.

"For bravery of the highest order," droned

the president with a surprisingly robotlike voice. "Above and beyond the call of duty, etc, etc. We Kerboskians will always be grateful to ..." Here the president stopped and consulted his cue cards. "Mr. Robbie Packford, otherwise known as the species Campythronagithicus Fabutali."

He stared at me. "You are a mythological creature!" he exclaimed. "I didn't believe you existed until this minute." The president pinched my scales. "You feel real enough," he said doubtfully.

Dr. Freedelhum touched the president's arm. "Excuse me, Mr. President, the ceremony."

"Ceremony?" said the president, looking rather confused.

"Yes," whispered Dr. Freedelhum, "it's all on the cue cards."

"But we're awarding the highest decoration in all of Kerbosky to a mythological creature whose name I can barely pronounce."

"I am actually a boy, Mr. President," I interrupted. "I only look like a Campythronagithicus Fabutali."

"A boy?" said the president, more confused than ever.

"From Earth," I added, "third planet from the Sun in one of those far arms of the Milky Way."

The president was dumbfounded. "Why are we awarding the highest honor in Kerbosky to a mythological creature who is actually an alien? This is unheard of," he sputtered.

All this time we were surrounded by a swarm of robots who kept asking Dr. Freedelhum how he wanted his pizza done and was that to go or to dine in.

Dr. Freedelhum dismissed them with a wave of his hand and grabbed his pince-nez back from being polished for the fourteenth time. He whispered rather loudly in the president's ear, "It's all on the cue cards, sir. Even if the boy is an alien and looks like a monster, he did save Kerbosky from the robots."

The robots looked offended at these words. But they did not for an instant stop trying to serve us, up on the raised platform, as well as the thousands of guests waiting impatiently for me to be given the Medal of Honor so that they could try out the newest rage on Kerbosky, Earth pizza.

One robot held a large pizza in front of Dr. Freedelhum's nose. "With everything, dear doctor?" he droned.

"Not now! After the ceremony," Dr. Freedelhum said. The robots withdrew the pizza. The president followed it longingly with his eyes.

"With everything, you say?" he asked.

By this time even my monster saliva was beginning to run down the corners of my jaws. "Maybe I'll just take a slice of pizza instead of the medal," I offered.

Jamie stepped up to the dais. "No, Robbie, you deserve the medal. If you hadn't changed the Master Ordinance . . ."

"We would never have tasted pizza again," finished Dr. Freedelhum. "And to think of it, our little plan did work out well, in fact, very well. If you hadn't tried to complete the invincibility formula on Earth, Jamie, then . . ."

"I would never have drunk it," I finished.

Dr. Freedelhum smiled. "And you would never have become Campy, and if you had never become Campy, then you wouldn't have been able to become invisible and penetrate the Nerve Center and . . ."

"Etcetera, etcetera," concluded Jamie.

"Exactly," agreed Dr. Freedelhum happily. "I'll raise a cappuccino to that!"

I scrunched up my forehead scales in consternation. My scaly snout had almost undone us, I thought. What would you call it, success by a snout, in spite of a snout?

At last the president began the presentation again, but not before remarking how irregular the whole affair was. By the time I got my medal I wished only for a piece of pizza. The president pinned, or rather stuck, the medal on one of my scales. Naturally, it was blood red and didn't look a bit like a medal. It had some yellow squiggles on it in Kerboskian about being a hero. The kids in Mrs. Cardwell's class back on Earth were not going to be impressed.

The president finished his speech. He bowed to me and I back to him. Unfortunately, my fang bumped into his forehead, not doing any serious damage, but it did cause about a hundred robots to swarm around the president offering him bandages, cushions, smelling salts and even his favorite teddy to hold in case he should faint.

"At last," said Dr. Freedelhum, wiping his brow. "Now for the pizza."

In a flash, robots with pizza were everywhere, with every variety Earth had dreamed up and a few new ones, too.

Jamie shook my hand. "Kerbosky must seem like a crazy place to you, Robbie, but we're used to it. And you really are a hero. You really did save Kerbosky from the robots."

"Let's have pizza," I said, "and then get me back to being human and back to Earth before I flunk out of grade six."

Jamie clapped me on the scales and we noshed down on the best pizza I had ever tasted. I bet the whole planet smelled like pizza for days after that party.

About a thousand robots shook my hand and reminded me how nice they were. The last one held my claws in its metallic hands longer than the others. Then, staring deeply into my beady red eyes with all six of its yellow eyes atop all six of its silver eyestalks, it winked. Six winks! It all happened so fast that I couldn't be sure it had happened at all. Those six winking eyestalks seemed to be giving me a message.

Maybe on Kerbosky things weren't quite as normal as they seemed.

While I was still thinking this over, Jamie said, "I've been working on the formula on the computer. I think I've got it just right. If we go back to the spaceship, I can make you human again."

I dropped my pizza. "Let's go!" I exclaimed.

Jamie and Dr. Freedelhum and I stood still as the sapphire blue light enveloped us and our molecules shimmered and faded. The Kerboskians didn't notice that their guest of honor had left the scene. I remembered the video clip that Dr. Freedelhum had showed me of them all being slaves to the robots. I guessed they must have forgotten that, too. My last memory of Kerbosky was of thousands of mouths chewing and strings of pizza cheese everywhere, and, of course, thousands and thousands of robots offering more pizza, and more and more.

The whole of Kerbosky will have to go on a diet, I thought. Maybe Aunt Rose's tofu wasn't so bad after all.

Chapter Fourteen

"It's pretty simple, really," Jamie said once we were back aboard the spaceship. "The same formula, only in reverse and . . ."

"Presto," finished Dr. Freedelhum. "You'll be Robbie Packford once again, human boy. But I have gotten rather fond of your present self. There can be something a bit fetching about Campys. If you would consider staying in your present body just for a little while longer, we could find out more about your species."

Jamie frowned.

"No way," I growled.

"Just a thought," said Dr. Freedelhum, "but perhaps my continued investigations of Earth food will be my next great scientific coup."

"Franchisable!" Jamie added.

Dr. Freedelhum wiped his pince-nez on his lab coat. "Exactly," he said.

All the time we were talking, our tiny spacecraft was whipping through hyperspace towards that out-of-the-way arm of the Milky Way where an insignificant sun shone on nine circling planets. Right now I was only interested in the blue one that was my home.

Jamie held up a small vial of liquid. "Here it is," he announced. "It's perfect."

"Are you absolutely and totally certain?" I demanded.

"Of course," answered Jamie. "I've double- and triple-checked on the computer."

I took the vial in my claws and peered at the green liquid.

"Bottoms up," said Dr. Freedelhum.

It was either drink or remain in my monster form forever, but Jamie's first effort left me doubtful. Who knew what I might turn into after drinking this stuff? Dr. Freedelhum and Jamie were eyeing me expectantly.

"Here goes," I said and downed the green liquid in one gulp. At least it tasted okay, kind of like lime pop.

Jamie held a mirror up to my snout, and my beady red eyes stared at themselves. Nothing happened. I stood still for a moment, watching my long purple tongue wipe the last drops of the green liquid from my leathery lips. I don't want to look this way forever, I moaned to myself. How could I have a life? Girls didn't want to go out with boys who had fangs and claws and dripped saliva down their scaly chins.

Suddenly, things started to happen. I felt hot. I felt cold. I began to itch all over. Then I sneezed a gigantic monster sneeze. When I opened my eyes, Jamie had collapsed in the corner and the mirror was shattered into a thousand pieces. "Are you okay?" I growled, but Jamie leaped to his feet.

"It's working," he shouted. "You're changing before my eyes." I looked at my claws. They were reforming themselves into fingers, human fingers. My growly voice went up about an octave. My fangs began to recede into my jaws.

"Quick, another mirror," I cried out. Dr. Freedelhum hurried to get one, and as I stared at myself, the last bit of red faded from my eyes and they became blue. I even had my old glasses on. I was wearing the same shirt and jeans that I had on so long ago when this whole thing started. I felt my skin. It was warm and soft like human skin. I felt my hair. It was kind of messy and tousled, but it was mine, my very own hair. I smiled at myself and looked at my even teeth inside my mouth. "Wow!" I said at last. "I really am me."

Dr. Freedelhum and Jamie smiled. "A scientific success, Jamie, my boy. Do you think you could repeat it?"

"Not today," Jamie and I both shrieked at him.

"Can you get me back to Earth?" I asked breathlessly.

"Just putting the spaceship in orbit around your moon, then teleportation coming right up," said Jamie, fiddling with the controls.

"Wait a minute," I demanded. "When I read about space travel, a whole lot more time passes on Earth than during space travel. I think Einstein said that. Am I going to get back to Earth just in time to see my friends all old and wrinkled?"

"Not to worry," said Dr. Freedelhum. "We can make some adjustments."

"I need to get back to grade six. I need to finish my socials project. Mrs. Cardwell deducts marks for lateness."

Who knew how late my report on ancient Greece was going to be? Weeks, months, years? Mrs. Cardwell could be retired by the time I returned and I would forever be known as the boy who disappeared in the middle of grade six without finishing his report on ancient Greece. Maybe by the time I returned, grade six boys would be writing reports on ancient civilizations in the twenty-first century. I'd never know who won the Stanley Cup. I always rooted for the Vancouver Canucks, although they were headed for the basement of the league the last time I heard.

"Don't worry, " Jamie cautioned, showing me a program on the computer. "You know how humans have discovered that time is curved. You can nip in and out of it quite easily. It's not fixed, as in just going forward."

I nodded my head doubtfully. Einstein again. I might have been a math whiz for grade six, but quantum physics was out of my league.

"If that's true," I demanded, "then who

is going to win the Stanley Cup?"

Jamie fiddled with the computer controls. "Vancouver Canucks," he announced.

"That proves you're wrong," I shouted. "They would have had to win seven straight games even to get into the play-offs. Why the statistical probability of that is . . ."

Jamie fiddled with the computer program again. "Four billion to one," he said.

About the same as the number of robots with atomic vaporizers who had been poised to take over the universe, I thought.

Jamie motioned to me. "You see, I can just program in the day we were in your basement experimenting with the formula, and then I can send you back at exactly the same instant. You'll still have time to finish your socials project."

"Can't that machine whip me up my project plus one of those relief maps, the kind you make out of salt and flour and water?"

Jamie shook his head. "We're in orbit now. The time will be exactly right for teleporting in two minutes and fifty-six seconds."

"Please move towards the teleporter," said Dr. Freedelhum. "It's been great knowing you and I'll never forget Earth pizza."

"Wait," I said. "What am I going to tell everyone on Earth about what happened to me?"

"What's to tell?" asked Jamie. "You came home after school and went down to the basement. That's it."

"After all that's happened, that's IT?" I shouted, thinking of four billion not-nice robots ready to take over the universe; thinking of me, the Campythronagithicus Fabutali, ready to chow down on any fresh meat that moved and whose atoms narrowly missed being blasted all over space.

"I'm afraid so," said Dr. Freedelhum with a smile, glancing at his watch. "Two minutes, nine seconds."

"What about you, Jamie?" I demanded. "You were in Mrs. Cardwell's class, too."

Jamie shrugged. "You know how it is. Students come and students go."

Dr. Freedelhum was edging me towards the teleporter. "Begin the countdown on my mark," he said calmly, as if this sort of thing happened to them every day. Who knew, on a crazy place like Kerbosky, it just might.

Jamie shook my hand. "You're a good friend, Robbie," he said, "and don't forget, you really did save Kerbosky."

The blue light began to envelop me. Jamie smiled and waved.

"Thanks for the pizza, Robbie. It's a great contribution to Kerboskian civilization," Dr. Freedelhum said, just as my molecules began to fade out.

Chapter Fifteen

Sure enough, I was standing in my own basement. In my own house. This was amazing. My molecules were still me. I felt exactly like Robbie Packford except for one thing. I had this strange craving for meat. A rare steak would sure hit the spot, I thought. Normally I didn't even like steak, being more of a hamburger guy, myself. I shook my head to rid myself of the picture of the grilled steak that danced in front of my eyes.

I trudged up the stairs and glanced out the window. My sister was still skipping outside with her friends, the whiners. I heard a car in the driveway. Mom was home! Say, wasn't this where I had come in? I started to feel like I was in a movie — you know — the ones that play all day and you're in a big rush and you come in late so you have to stay for the beginning of the next repeat.

Mom came in the door, loaded down with two bags of groceries. I grabbed her, bags and all, and gave her a ferocious hug.

"Mom," I said, "let me help you put away the food."

She stared at me in disbelief as I started putting away cereal , cheese, luncheon meat. I reminded myself not to drool over the meat. You'll be totally normal again soon, I repeated to myself.

"What's come over you, Robbie?" my mother demanded as I gave her another hug. She felt my forehead after I promised to clean up my room right after I finished the supper dishes tonight. "Are you sure you're feeling well?" she asked. "You're not in any trouble at school are you?"

"Everything's fine, Mom," I said, "absolutely fine. Our house is sure nice and I really like the color of the sky today. Blue, just blue."

Mom shook her head. "Dinner is in one hour," she said. "Tell your sister."

I nodded. "I'm going out for a few minutes,

but I'll be back in time to set the table."

My mom was speechless. Even I had to admit that this wasn't the usual Robbie, all this helpful stuff. It would probably wear off along with my desire for raw meat. I went outside to check things out. The whole street was totally, deliciously normal. My sister even insulted me as I went by, and one of her friends stuck her tongue out at me. Boy, that felt good.

I walked up the crescent, only to see Darryl, Peter and Chris coming along. Usually I went the other way. Too bad I couldn't program that Be Nice Master Ordinance into those three. I could just imagine them carrying my books, making me snacks and calling me Master.

"Hey, math boy," Chris called out in a mocking voice. That's what they called me. Being the fastest multiplier in grade six was not the best basis for lasting friendship and popularity.

"Hey, guys," I answered, almost, but not quite, glad to see them. I had to test this out. "Where's the new kid, Jamie?" I asked.

They laughed. "That weirdo. Moved away to some town called Kerbosky."

"I guess that's pretty far away," I said.

Darryl laughed. "You could say that. How about in another galaxy?" I stared. Then I saw his index finger pointing towards his temple and turning, the sign for crazy.

"Maybe you want to move there, too," said Chris, standing right up against me. Unfortunately, he had been one of the first of the grade sixers to experience a growth spurt, and mine had shown no signs of beginning.

"That's too bad," I said. "I was starting to like him."

"You would," they chorused. "You two have a lot in common."

"I think you might be right," I said. Chris's hot breath was steaming up my glasses. "Jamie knew a lot about statistics," I went on. "And a lot about space."

Chris was so close to me he was almost standing on my toes. "You've got a lot to say for a geeky math squirt."

I squared my shoulders. "How 'bout those Vancouver Canucks?" I said.

"Right," said Darryl. "Trust you to back a loser."

"They're going to win the Stanley Cup," I blurted out, remembering what Jamie had said, even if the odds were four billion to one.

Great guffaws greeted my words. "They'll be dead last."

"You're as nutty as that geek, Jamie, who said he was from outer space."

"Maybe the Vancouver Canucks should go to outer space."

"And find a league they can win in against little green men."

Then a comment caught my attention. "You want to make a bet on the Stanley Cup right now?" demanded Darryl. He dug into his jeans pocket and pulled out a handful of change and a crumpled bill. "I've got my allowance right here." He pushed the fistful of money into my face and for an instant I wished I had claws and fangs again. "Wanna bet?" he demanded.

Now all three of them were right in my personal space. I looked away. "Naw," I said at last. "The odds are four billion to one against."

I walked back up the pavement towards my house. The three of them watched me go. Chris made the same sign for crazy next to his temple that Darryl had made when we talked about Jamie. I was in good company. Jamie had turned out to be a pretty good friend. I missed him.

And I sure wish I had taken Darryl up on that bet about the Canucks. It was the odds that got me down. I should have bet them all their allowance for the next month. Then I could have been a Kerboskian hero with a lot of spending money.

As it was, I put the medal in my special keepsake box with my old coins and my silent dog whistle. If Jamie and Dr. Freedelhum ever come back to Earth and give me odds on another Stanley Cup, well, I'll clean up!

Heather Sander haunted the public library as a child and still reads children's books every chance she gets. While *Robbie Packford — Alien Monster* is her first published book, she started writing stories years ago for her now-grown children. Heather is an elementary school counselor who lives with her husband in Victoria, British Columbia.

Look for the next Robbie Packford story, *Make Mine With Everything*, in bookstores in March 2004. Here is a selection from the opening chapter:

I wandered around the playground, keeping away from Chris and company. My sister, Mary, had gone off to play with her bratty friends. They were into skipping these days. I walked across the grass. I could have done a couple of laps for the cross-country, but I wandered in behind the music portable instead.

It was then I heard it. "Psst," someone said in a stage whisper. "Robbie, over here."

I looked around. That whisper sounded familiar. I started to shiver, even though it was a warm spring morning.

"Up here," whispered the voice. I looked up into the great Garry oak above me. Now, climbing the Garry oak in the schoolyard was a big no-no. It was a heritage tree from the time when only First Nations people lived here. Being up in it meant an instant lecture from the principal plus several lunch hours of garbage duty.

"Up here," said the voice again.

I squinted up through the sun and the spring leaves. My jaw dropped.

"It's me, Jamie," said the voice, and the boy in the tree, who was about my size with reddish brown hair instead of dirty blond and hazel eyes instead of blue, waved at me. He was smiling. He beckoned me to come closer to the gnarled trunk of the old oak. "I'm back," he said.

At that instant the bell rang. I hesitated.

Jamie did look real. He was exactly how I remembered him when he first came to school, exactly the way I remembered when it began to get real crazy.

I pinched myself. "Ouch!"

Jamie slithered down the trunk of the tree.

"You're not real, right?" I said. "I know I'm dreaming you. It's time for me to wake up and get into school."

By this time the schoolyard had emptied. Even the few stragglers from the basketball court had gathered up their ball and disappeared through the big double school doors. The schoolyard was silent.

Jamie clapped me on the arm. "Of course you're not dreaming, Robbie," he said. "I beamed down a few minutes ago. I figured you'd be along to school, so I was waiting."

I touched the sleeve of Jamie's jacket. It felt like real cloth.

"Are you going to be in Mrs. Cardwell's

class again?" I asked. "Maybe we could be partners in the science fair."

Jamie shook his head. "I've got my own school in Kerbosky," he said. "I even have a private robot tutor."

"You just dropped in for a visit from another galaxy?" I asked, becoming suspicious.

"Yes and no," answered Jamie.

"Yes and no?" I repeated.

When Jamie smiled, I remembered how much I had liked him as a friend, even though he had only been at Clover Elementary for a few days.

"I'm glad to see you," he said, "and we need your help."

"We?"

Jamie nodded. "Dr. Freedelhum and I. There is a bit of a crisis on Kerbosky. The president's been kidnapped."

I remembered the president of Kerbosky. He had presented me with the medal that was now in my keepsake box. He had seemed more interested in pizza than in me. I looked at Jamie doubtfully.

"He's being held for ransom in suspended animation," Jamie continued, "and time is running out to save him."